KLOOZ

The Great Snake Swindle

by J. Banscherus

translated by Daniel C. Baron

illustrated by Ralf Butschkow

Librarian Reviewer
Marci Peschke
Librarian, Dallas Independent School District
MA Education Reading Specialist, Stephen F. Austin State University
Learning Resources Endorsement, Texas Women's University

Reading Consultant
Mary Evenson
Middle School Teacher, Edina Public Schools, MN
MA in Education, University of Minnesota

STONE ARCH BOOKS
Minneapolis San Diego

First published in the United States in 2007
by Stone Arch Books,
151 Good Counsel Drive, P.O. Box 669,
Mankato, Minnesota 56002
www.stonearchbooks.com

First published by Arena Books,
Rottendorfer str. 16, D-97074,
Würzburg, Germany

Library of Congress Cataloging-in-Publication Data
Banscherus, Jürgen.
    [Grosse Schlangenzauber. English]
    The Great Snake Swindle / by J. Banscherus; translated by Daniel C.
Baron; illustrated by Ralf Butschkow.
    p. cm. — (Pathway Books = Klooz)
    Summary: While celebrating his eleventh birthday with his mother
and his friend Olga, Klooz relates the case that started his detective
career, which involved magic balls, and a boy named Snake who was his
best friend.
    ISBN-13: 978-1-59889-340-3 (library binding)
    ISBN-10: 1-59889-340-8 (library binding)
    ISBN-13: 978-1-59889-435-6 (paperback)
    ISBN-10: 1-59889-435-8 (paperback)
    [1. Friendship—Fiction 2. Swindlers and swindling—Fiction.
3. Mystery and detective stories.] I. Baron, Daniel C. II. Butschkow,
Ralf, ill. III. Title.
PZ7.B22927Gr 2007
[Fic]—dc22   2006027193

Art Director: Heather Kindseth
Graphic Designer: Kay Fraser

1 2 3 4 5 6 12 11 10 09 08 07

Printed in the United States of America

KLOOZ

The Great
Snake Swindle

Table of contents

TOP SECRET

CHAPTER 1

Birthday Dinner

Two weeks ago I turned eleven. The night before my birthday I was so excited, I could hardly sleep. Eleven years old! Wow, who could believe it?

When I woke up, my mom gave me my present. I got a detective's vest with seventeen pockets, and bright red sneakers that everybody in school would envy.

"Do you like your gifts?" my mom asked.

"You bet!" I replied. Then I put on my new shoes and the vest.

In the vest pockets, I put Carpenter's chewing gum, a note pad, pens, a magnifying glass, and everything else that a successful detective needs to solve cases.

As I was about to leave, my mom stopped me.

"Your dad wrote you a letter," she said. She pulled an envelope out of her jacket pocket.

"Yeah, right," I said.

In the past few months I had only gotten phone calls from my dad. And then the conversations were mostly like, "How's it going? Good, see you later."

Mom handed me the envelope. Inside was a birthday card.

When I opened it, it played "Happy Birthday to You."

Mom made a face at the song. I wasn't too thrilled with the card either. At least my dad remembered my birthday. Last year he forgot it completely. That really bothered me.

My dad wrote that the card had a secret compartment and that I, as a detective, would have little trouble finding it.

I got busy right away. My dad was right. It didn't take me much time at all. You had to fold the card a certain way and the secret compartment opened.

Inside I found a folded fifty-dollar bill! It was the most money I'd ever had in my life!

After school, I stopped at Olga's
newspaper stand. That's where I always
buy my Carpenter's chewing gum. Olga
knows I need the gum in order to think.

"Happy birthday!" she cried when she saw me. "Don't go away!"

Then she disappeared into her newspaper stand. When she came back, she pushed a little package over the counter.

Just like last year and the year before, she had wrapped it in green paper with little bears on it.

Come on, I was eleven! She should use wrapping paper with NASCAR racers or space shuttles.

After I opened the package, all was forgiven.

Olga had given me eleven packs of Carpenter's chewing gum, one for every year.

"Only the best for you, Klooz!" she said happily.

"Thanks," I said quickly. I put a pack of gum in my pocket and I felt the fifty-dollar bill there.

If I wanted to, I could have bought fifty more packs of gum.

That wouldn't be a bad idea, but suddenly I had a better one.

"Are you free tonight?" I asked Olga.

"For you, always."

"I want to invite you and my mom for ice cream," I said. "At seven o'clock at Vinnie's. Does that sound okay?"

"Me? You want to take me, too?" Olga said. Then Olga said quietly, "It would be an honor, Klooz."

* * *

So a couple of hours later we were sitting together in Vinnie's ice cream parlor. "What I always wanted to know, Klooz, was how you became a detective in the first place," Olga said.

My mom said, "What I would like to know is when you will finally quit being a detective."

Even though I've solved lots of cases, my mom is not happy about me being a detective. She thinks that it affects my grades. Maybe she's right.

"You want to know how it all started?" I asked Olga.

"Well," I said, "it happened like this. I call it the case of the great snake swindle."

CHAPTER 2

Dexter or Snake?

Unlike most of the detectives in this city, I work alone.

A few years ago that wasn't true. I had a friend.

Actually, Dexter was more like a twin brother.

We liked the same comics and hated the same food. And we were both interested in everything that had to do with thieves, kidnappers, and swindlers.

We even
decided to open
our own detective
agency. We knew
we would become
the most famous
detectives in
the world.

We are the champions !!!

SHERLOCK HOLMES

But then the day came
that changed everything.
It was a Friday and it
was raining.

When I went into the kitchen that
morning, my mom was sitting at the
window, crying. I had never seen my
mom cry before.

"What's the matter?" I asked.

She sniffled. "Dad is gone."

I looked at the clock. "Of course he's gone," I said. "He has to be at work at eight o'clock."

She wiped the tears from her eyes. "He isn't coming back," she mumbled.

"You mean, ever?" I asked.

"Never again," Mom answered.

It was like the world had suddenly stopped turning. And when it started to turn again, everything had changed.

My parents had argued a lot lately. They had argued with me, too. It didn't mean that I was going to leave.

"Is he crazy?" I yelled. I didn't cry. Not yet. I ran into my dad's office and tipped over his bookshelves.

Then I tipped over his desk and chair and the file cabinet. I would have thrown everything out the window if Mom hadn't come into the room. She looked at the mess I made. Then she dropped onto the floor between all the tipped furniture and started laughing.

That made me feel a little better. Laughing is better than crying, I guess. "I have to go to school," I said.

She stood up. "You don't have to go to school today if you don't want to."

I shook my head. "I think I should go."

My mom wrapped her arms around me.

"You and I will be okay," she said.

"Of course we will," I replied. But I didn't cry. No way. Not a single tear because of Dad.

At the corner Dexter was waiting for me. Dexter's parents usually made him dress like a nerd and wear his hair parted on the side of his head. On Sundays, he even had to wear a bow tie. He looked like a guy on the TV news.

Whenever I talked to him about how he dressed, Dexter always said, "Who cares about the way someone dresses?"

But that day everything was different. His hair was standing like a cactus on his head. He was wearing jeans and a bright green sweatshirt. To be honest, his nerdy clothes looked better.

"Hey," he said.

Dexter's voice sounded different. It sounded sad.

"My dad left," I said. When Dexter didn't react, I went on, "He left for good."

"My dad, too," Dexter mumbled.

No way! Dexter had to be kidding.

"You're lying!" I yelled.

"It's true," he said. "He moved out yesterday."

"Wow! My dad moved out this morning," I said.

"Wow," he said.

We didn't say another word until we got to school. We each knew how the other felt.

It was good to have a friend like Dexter.

Two months later, Dexter and his mom moved and he switched schools.

We still saw each other on weekends. Sometimes we talked on the phone or met at the mall.

But we talked less and less. Something else had changed.

Since his mom and dad split up, Dexter had lost interest in detective work.

Whenever I talked to him about our agency, he just yawned. He said he was interested in other things. What those other things were he never told me.

One morning my mom said, "Dexter hasn't been over in a while."

She was right. We hadn't seen each other for two weeks.

The last time we got together was a Saturday. We went to see a movie.

That Saturday, Dexter had been pretty quiet. He just said that his mom had a new boyfriend. When I asked whether he liked the guy, Dexter just shrugged. The movie we saw was not very good.

My mom asked me, "Did you and Dexter have a fight?"

My mom's question pulled me from my thoughts.

"Nah," I answered.

"Then what's wrong?" she asked.

"I don't know, Mom, really!"

The next day, on the way to school, I decided to call Dexter that afternoon and get together with him. After all, he was still my friend and you shouldn't let friendships die.

When school was over, I walked over to the Cool Stuff ice cream parlor. I was surprised to see Dexter there.

He wasn't alone. He was with three boys.

"I'm glad that I ran into you," I said. "I was going to call you anyway."

One of the three boys got in between
us. "What's this little guy want?" he
asked in an unfriendly tone.

Dexter pushed him out of the way.
"Leave him alone, Mike."

"Do you have time this afternoon?" I
asked him.

"This afternoon? Nah," he said.

"What about this weekend?" I asked.

Dexter looked at his watch. It looked new. I had never seen it before.

"Give me a call, okay?" he said.

"What's up, Snake?" one of the boys said. "We've got to go."

"Snake?" I said in surprise. "Why are they calling you Snake?"

He grinned. "Well, my name is Dexter Blake, and Blake rhymes with Snake. Get it?"

"Okay, I get it," I said.

It was still weird. I'd never thought of rhyming snake with Blake.

I didn't see him that weekend, the next weekend, or the one after that.

Whenever I called, his mom always said, "Dexter isn't here right now. Dexter is with his friends."

After a while, I gave up. In any case, I hardly had time to think about Dexter, because that's when the first magic ball appeared at my school.

It all started when a kid from my class named Sean pulled me aside at recess. He opened his hand and showed me a small plastic ball.

"It's one of those magic balls," Sean whispered.

I laughed. "That thing is supposed to be a magic ball?"

Sean nodded. "Almost everybody has one," he said.

Somehow I had missed out.

"What does a magic ball do?" I asked.

Quiet
reCess
Corner
PSSST!

Sean smiled and looked around to make sure no one was watching us. Then he leaned in close to me.

"When your mom is cooking dinner, you just drop the ball into the food and then wish for something," he said.

"And I'll get what I wish for?" I asked. He nodded.

"Always?" I asked.

"Not always. Only at Christmas or for your birthday," Sean answered.

"Yeah right," I said, bored.

Suddenly Sean got really angry. "Did I get a TV for my birthday or not? It even has a DVD player. The magic balls work! I have proof!"

"And where would I get one of these magic balls?" I asked.

"After school some boys come here," said Sean. "If you want, I'll show you who they are. They sell them for ten dollars a ball. Of course a magic ball works only one time. Then you have to buy a new one."

"Of course," I replied.

Ten dollars per ball? That was a fortune!

When Dexter hears about this, I thought, I'll bet he'll want to investigate it with me.

At home, I tried calling him again. This time I was lucky.

"I've got a case for us," I said. "And it's big. It's huge. It's gigantic!"

"Ah," he said.

"So, you want to help me work on it?" I asked.

"Nah," he replied.

"Why not?"

"I have better things to do," he replied.

"Like what?" I wanted to know.

"That's none of your business," he said. Then he hung up.

So that's how things were. Another person in my life was leaving me. Dexter turned into Snake, and now we weren't friends anymore. That was that.

Oh well. I had better things to do than worry. I had detective fever.

CHAPTER 3

Selling Magic

The next morning I was sick. At least that's what my mom thought. She felt my forehead and cried, "You are hot!"

"Of course I'm hot," I replied. "I'm the hottest detective around."

"I mean, you feel hot," she said.

"It's detective fever," I said.

"You're staying in bed," she said firmly.

Good Morning.
I am your talking thermometer. Your current temperature is 100 degrees. Thanks for using me, I will now shut down. Beep!

When she took my temperature it was only one hundred degrees.

"Please, Mom," I said. "I want to go to school."

She raised her eyebrows. "You want to go to school?" she asked.

I nodded. She thought for a moment and then shook her head.

"You're not going. If you rest today, then you'll get well enough to go back tomorrow," she said.

"What about you?" I asked. "You have to go to work."

"You'll have to stay alone. But I am going to call you every hour, okay? I'll be back home at two o'clock sharp."

She went into the kitchen, brought me soup and crackers, and placed the phone next to my bed.

A few minutes later I heard the front door shut.

Even if I were at school, I couldn't be working on the case of the magic balls.

I would be sitting in class. So I decided to get a little sleep.

I woke up when the phone rang. It was my mom.

"How is it going?" she asked.

"Good," I mumbled, still half asleep.

"And your fever?"

I felt my forehead. It was ice cold. "I don't have one anymore," I said.

"Stay in bed anyway, okay? I'll call you later."

Then she hung up.

After I ate a couple of crackers and had some soup, I got up.

I felt a little wobbly.

I figured it was because I'd been in bed for so long.

I went to the living room, fell into the most comfortable chair, and turned on the TV.

At noon my mom called for the fourth time to see if I was still alive. Then, when she hung up, I left the apartment and ran to school.

When I got to school, I hid in a bush behind the bicycle stand. Even though people wouldn't see me, I was in the middle of the action. If magic balls were going to be bought and sold here, I'd be able to see it happen.

The bell rang. Before the first kids came running through the school gate, three boys on skateboards stopped right in front of the bicycle stand. Their baseball caps were pulled low over their faces so that you couldn't recognize them.

The school door opened and a wave of kids rushed out of it. One of the three boys put his fingers to his mouth and whistled so loud that it nearly blew my ears off. Some of the kids turned to look at the three boys. Sean from my class walked over.

"Give me another one," Sean said as he pulled a ten-dollar bill from his pocket. One of the boys took the money while another one reached into his pocket and pulled out a magic ball. And so it went: money, magic ball, money, magic ball.

Where do kids get so much money? I knew that most of them didn't get more than two dollars a week from their parents in allowance.

After the last student left, the three boys got on their skateboards and were about to leave.

"Wait!" I called.

The three turned around, their faces still hidden by the caps. I had the funny feeling I had seen them before.

"What do you want?" the biggest of the three asked.

"Are you selling magic balls?" I asked

The three looked at each other but said nothing.

"I want one," I said, "but I don't know if I have enough money."

"A ball costs ten dollars," one of them said. "Bring the money tomorrow."

"Ten dollars," I mumbled. "That's pretty expensive."

The three laughed. "If you want a PlayStation and the magic ball helps you get it, then ten dollars is pretty cheap," one of them said.

Then they left.

On the way home I took my time.

I felt a little tired. I probably had some kind of stupid bacteria running around in my body.

When I walked past the newsstand near my house, I got a craving for chewing gum. Until that day, I only got cravings for milk, which I drank by the gallon.

There was nothing going on at the newsstand. The woman behind the counter smiled at me.

"What can I get for you?" she asked.

"A pack of chewing gum."

"Any certain kind?" she asked.

"It doesn't matter," I said.

She laid a pack on the counter. "This is Carpenter's chewing gum. It's the best there is," she said with a funny grin.

"How much is it?" I asked

"One dollar." Then she added, "You'll never want any other kind."

I put my money on the counter and was about to go when she stopped me.

"What's your name?" she asked.

Normally I would have just told her my name. But now I was a real detective.

I was just like Sherlock Holmes and a real detective needs a special name.

"Klooz," I said.

"Klooz?" she asked.

"Klooz," I repeated. My last name suddenly seemed the perfect detective name.

"Just Klooz," I said.

She stuck out her hand for me to shake. "My name is Olga," she said with a grin. "Just Olga."

After I left, I stuck a piece of Carpenter's chewing gum in my mouth.

At first it tasted like any other chewing gum.

But after a while I noticed that the weakness in my body was gone.

My arms and legs felt strong again. It felt like some kind of fog had been lifted from my head and I could think clearly again.

So that's how I met Olga. The boys from my class laugh at me when they see me talking to her, but they don't have a clue. If it weren't for Olga I wouldn't be the detective that I am today.

She is the smartest woman in the
world, even though sometimes she
acts like she can't count to three. With
Carpenter's chewing gum I can think
and plan and solve cases. The gum also
helps get rid of boredom, angry moms,
mean teachers, and yes, even fear.

Every detective knows fear, whether
he admits it or not.

CHAPTER 4

Mothballs

At home my mom met me at the door. I never dreamed that she would be home already.

She grabbed me by the arm. "You cannot disappear on me like that!" she yelled. "What were you thinking?

"I needed some chewing gum," I said.

She brushed her hair out of her eyes. "Next time you call me," she said. "Do you know how scared I was?"

"I'll call," I said.

"And now go to bed!"

The next morning I felt great. Maybe it was the Carpenter's. I felt strong enough to rip trees out of the ground. Maybe not the oak tree in front of our house, but at least the birch tree behind it.

Later I went to the basement and got the hammer out of the toolbox. Back in my room I broke my piggy bank. I found only seven dollars. That wasn't enough.

"Can I borrow three dollars?" I asked my mom at breakfast. "You can take it out of my allowance."

"What do you need the money for?" she asked.

I was ready for her question.

"It's for a magic ball," I explained.

"A magic ball?" she asked.

I nodded.

To my surprise, she gave me the money without asking any other questions. I put the money in my pocket with the seven dollars from my piggy bank and went to school.

* * *

When the final bell rang at the end of the day, I ran outside.

There they were. The three boys stood at the bicycle stand. Just like the day before, the biggest of the three whistled and at least twenty kids ran up to him. The magic ball business seemed like it was getting better every day.

I was the last in line. In order to stop my nervousness, I stuck a piece of gum in my mouth. That helped. In no time I felt peaceful.

Finally it was my turn.

As the boy tried to take the money from my hand, I pulled my hand back.

"What happens if the magic ball doesn't work?" I asked. "Do I get my money back?"

"Up to now every ball has worked," the smallest of the three answered.

"Have you guys ever opened one up to look inside?" I asked.

The boys shook their heads. "Then they would lose their magic," answered the leader of the three. "So, what's it gonna be? Are you going to buy one or not?"

"Okay." I gave him the money and he pressed a magic ball into my hand. "Where do you guys get these balls anyway?" I asked before they took off.

"You're awfully curious," their leader said. Then they took off around the corner.

At home I got a saw from the toolbox and got to work. Even though I didn't believe in the magic power of the ball, I was still careful.

I wondered if an evil spirit would fly out of it and bite me on the nose.

Soon, two halves of the ball lay on the table. I don't know what I expected. I certainly didn't expect them to be completely empty.

Before I could hide the pieces of the ball, my mom came into the room. She picked up the two halves of the ball.

"Is this a magic ball?" she said.

I nodded.

"Why did you break it?"

"I wanted to know what was inside of it," I said.

"Did you find the mothball?" my mom asked.

"M-m-mothball?" I stuttered.

She put the halves back on the table. "Those are an old kind of mothball," said my mom. "You don't see them like this anymore. You paid three dollars for this?"

I was afraid to tell her that I'd really paid ten. Instead I said, "Thanks, Mom."

"For what?"

"You helped me a lot," I explained. "I am a private detective now, you know."

"Aha." She smiled. "And now you want to stop the people who sold you this mothball."

Olga may be smart, but Mom is really sharp. I wonder if I get my detective skills from her.

CHAPTER 5

The Empty Building

A few days later, my investigation led me to the hardware store around the corner from my house.

"Yes, we used to have a lot of those balls," said the woman behind the counter. "It was a special brand. We got a shipment of them a few weeks ago."

"A few weeks ago?" I asked. The wheels started to turn in my head. That's a sign that I am about to solve a case.

The woman nodded. "But the delivery was bad. All the balls were empty. We had to send them back," she said.

Her coworker joined us. "We got them ready to ship back, and then they just disappeared," she said.

"Stolen?" I asked.

"Probably," she said.

"And you have no idea who could have stolen them, or why?" I asked.

They both shook their heads. "Why are you interested in this?" the first woman asked.

"I'm a detective," I said.

"My name is Klooz," I added. "Just Klooz."

Now I had a plan. I needed to follow those magic ball sellers back to their hideout. So, after school I followed the three boys. They had skateboards, but luckily they weren't going very fast.

That day they had sold magic balls to at least forty kids, so the skateboarders were in a good mood.

At some point we walked down a dusty street surrounded by old apartment buildings. I had never been in this part of the city before.

When the three guys disappeared into one of the apartment buildings, I hid and thought about my next move. I put a piece of gum in my mouth.

Two ideas
came to me.

I could wait here
and see what happened.
Or I could go into
the building.

Finally, curiosity won.
I snuck over to the building
where the boys had
disappeared. The front
door was open. That made
things easier.

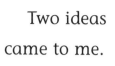

I took a deep breath
and went inside.

In the lobby it was dark. I could see
that no one lived here anymore. The doors
were open and the rooms were empty.

Quietly, I made my way back down stairs. When I reached the ground floor I heard laughter and voices. They seemed to come from a room far below me. When I opened a door marked Basement, the voices were louder and clearer.

"They are soooooo stupid!" I heard. Then I heard all four of them laugh.

Four? Why were there four of them now? Three boys had gone into the house but now I definitely heard four different voices.

I crept down the steep stairs into the basement and moved closer to the voices. After a while I peeked around the corner.

Yow! I was so shocked I almost yelled.

There was Dexter! He was sitting in an old red chair and was holding a wad of money. I couldn't believe it. Dexter was one of the bad guys. He had been my best friend. I had to come up with some way to stop them without bringing in the police or parents. But how?

Then I noticed a key in the door lock.

CHAPTER 6

Trapping a Snake

After I quickly locked the basement door, it took the four of them a while to recover from the shock. Then Dexter yelled, "Let us out of here!"

I didn't make a sound. I wanted the four of them to think a little. "Who are you?" Dexter yelled. "Why are you doing this?"

I put my mouth next to the door and said as quietly as possible, "Hello, Dexter. Pardon me. I mean, Snake."

"You?" I heard the voice of my old friend say. "Are you crazy? Open the door right now!"

"First, give me the balls," I said.

"The balls? You're crazy!"

I took a step back. "Okay then, I'll just call the police."

I heard whispers from behind the door. Then the balls came rolling through the gap.

"You're going to be sorry!" Dexter growled.

I didn't let him say anything more.

"Think about the police," I said.

One by one, two hundred balls rolled under the door. I figured that must be all of them.

I took my sweatshirt off, placed the empty mothballs on it, and took them outside. I found a storm drain and dropped the mothballs, one by one, into the drain.

Then I went back to the basement door. The four swindlers were really angry. "What else do you want from us?" Dexter asked.

"Two things," I said. "First you leave the kids from my school alone. And second, you give their money back. If you aren't at the bike stand tomorrow, I'll tell the police about everything."

I heard whispering. Then Dexter said, "Fine. Now open up."

Carefully, I shoved an old newspaper under the door. "What are we supposed to do with a newspaper?" Dexter complained. "Let us out!"

I dropped the key about two feet from the door. "You can go fishing with your newspaper. Good luck!" I yelled. Then I ran up the stairs and didn't stop running until I was home.

CHAPTER 7

Back at Dinner

Olga and Mom sat in the ice cream parlor and listened to my story. My mom even forgot to eat her ice cream.

"What a fantastic story," said Olga.

"You can say that again," my mom agreed. Then she turned to me. "So what happened to those four boys in the basement?" she asked.

I leaned back in my chair and grinned at her.

"They took about an hour to free themselves," I said. "Snake told me that later. He was the one who had stolen the mothballs from the store."

"And then?" Olga asked.

"Snake and his friends showed up at our school one more time," I said. "I had two of the balls and I showed the kids at school that they were empty. Some of them got their money back."

"Only some of them?" my mom said.

I nodded. "Most of the kids still didn't believe me. Take Sean, for example. He believed it was the magic ball that had brought him his TV."

Mom and Olga sat in silence. Then my mom said, shaking her head, "Some people want to be tricked."

Olga nodded. "You've got that right."

"It's too bad Dexter stopped being your friend," my mom said.

"Yeah," I said.

"Who knows," said my mom. "Maybe Dexter wouldn't have gone bad if you two were still friends."

I shrugged my shoulders.

I thought about Snake. I wondered if maybe he got into all that trouble because he couldn't handle his dad leaving him. Then I wondered why I didn't get into trouble. After all, my dad had left me, too. Why wasn't I out selling magic balls to silly kids?

Hmm. I guess detectives don't know everything.

About the Author

Jürgen Banscherus is a worldwide phenomenon. There are almost a million Klooz books in print, and they have been translated into Spanish, Danish, Thai, Chinese, and eleven other languages. He has worked as a newspaper writer, a research scientist, and a teacher. His first book for children was published in 1985. He lives with his family in Germany.

About the Illustrator

Ralf Butschkow was born in Berlin. He works as a freelance graphic designer and illustrator, and has published more than 50 books for children. Critics have praised his work as "thoroughly enjoyable," "creatively original," and "highly recommended."

Glossary

bacteria (bak-TEER-ee-uh)—tiny living things that live all around us; some bacteria can cause sickness

investigate (in-VES-tuh-gayt)—to search, to hunt for clues

mothball (MAWTH-bawl)—a tiny ball made of a substance that will keep moths away from clothing

suspicious (suss-PISH-us)—thinking or feeling that something is wrong; or acting in a way that makes people think something is wrong

swindle (SWIN-dul)—to cheat or trick someone out of their money

whine (WYN)—to complain in a childish or annoying way

Discussion Questions

1. Why did Dexter like being called Snake? Why did he like hanging around those other boys when he seemed to get along so well with Klooz?

2. At the end of the story, Klooz thinks about how he and Dexter were alike, but that they turned out differently. What turned Klooz into the kind of person who likes to help other people?

3. When Klooz bought a magic ball, why do you think he was hoping it would really work?

4. There are no snakes in this story, except for Dexter's new name. Why did the author give this book its title? What does a snake make you think of?

Writing Prompts

1. If the magic balls were real, and you had one, what would you wish for?

2. Klooz wonders, on page 52, if he gets his detective skills from his mom. Do you have any special skills or ways of doing things that you learned from other members of your family? Describe what they are.

3. Have you ever had a good friend like Dexter who then decided to act differently and hang out with other people? What happened? How did it make you feel? Did you become friends again? Would you, if you had the chance?

Internet Sites

Do you want to know more about subjects related to this book? Or are you interested in learning about other topics? Then check out FactHound, a fun, easy way to find Internet sites.

Our investigative staff has already sniffed out great sites for you!

Here's how to use FactHound:

1. Visit *www.facthound.com*

2. Select your grade level.

3. To learn more about subjects related to this book, type in the book's ISBN number: **1598893408**.

4. Click the **Fetch It** button.

FactHound will fetch the best Internet sites for you!